For Ann and Beth
with all my love

First published in 2000 by
David & Charles Children's Books,
Winchester House, 259-269 Old Marylebone Road,
London, NW1 5XJ

Text and Illustrations ©
Marie-Louise Fitzpatrick 2000

The right of Marie-Louise Fitzpatrick to be identified
as the author and illustrator of this work has been
asserted by her in accordance with the
Copyright, Designs, and Patents Act, 1988.
A CIP record for this title is
available from the British Library.

ISBN: 1-86233-150-2

Printed and bound in Belgium

Marie-Louise Fitzpatrick

Izzy and Skunk

David&Charles
Children's Books

A little girl called Izzy had

a skunk called Skunk.

'Isn't life wonderful?' said Skunk.

'But scary,' said Izzy.

Izzy was afraid of

shadows in the dark...

but Skunk wasn't.

Izzy was afraid

of falling down...

but Skunk wasn't.

Izzy was

afraid of

spiders…

but Skunk wasn't.

Izzy was afraid of making mistakes…

but Skunk wasn't.

Izzy got stage fright

at the school show...

but Skunk didn't.

Izzy thought

    the dark, scary

        woods were

            dark and scary.

So did Skunk.

One day, Skunk got lost.

'Skunk, Skunk,' called Izzy,

but there was no answer.

Izzy was going to have

to look for Skunk.

All by herself.

She looked under
the bed where
it was dark.
Skunk wasn't there.

She looked in the
attic where there
were spiders.
Skunk wasn't there.

She looked down the street
where there were shadows.
But there was no sign
of Skunk anywhere.

LOST
SKUNK

Then Izzy saw a crowd of people
standing by her garden wall.
'Look a skunk,' said a little boy,
pointing up into the tree.

'Not *a* skunk – *Skunk!'*

yelled Izzy.

'I'll save you, Skunk!'

she called.

Izzy climbed the tree.

Everyone watched.

She reached Skunk just

as he started to fall.

Everyone gasped.

Izzy caught Skunk.

Everyone clapped as

she climbed down.

Izzy was dirty, but she didn't care.

'Life is wonderful,' she said.

'But scary, too,' said Skunk.

'Don't worry, Skunk,' said Izzy.

'I'll take care of you.'

Other David & Charles Picture Books
for you to read and enjoy:

Harry and the Bucketful of Dinosaurs
Ian Whybrow • Adrian Reynolds
hardback: 1 86233 088 3
paperback: 1 86233 205 3

Tabitha's Terrifically Tough Tooth
Charlotte Middleton
hardback: 1 86233 172 3
paperback: 1 86233 267 3

Over in the Meadow
Jane Cabrera
hardback: 1 86233 137 5
paperback: 1 86233 280 0

The Show at Rickety Barn
Jemma Beeke • Lynne Chapman
hardback: 186233 142 1

Shoe Shoe Baby
Bernard Lodge • Katherine Lodge
hardback: 1 86233 189 8

David & Charles
Children's Books